Anonymous

Official Correspondence regarding the Existence of Coal and Iron in the Punjab

SALZWASSER
VERLAG

Anonymous

Official Correspondence regarding the Existence of Coal and Iron in the Punjab

Reprint of the original, first published in 1859.

1st Edition 2022 | ISBN: 978-3-37513-324-5

Verlag (Publisher): Salzwasser Verlag GmbH, Zeilweg 44, 60439 Frankfurt, Deutschland
Vertretungsberechtigt (Authorized to represent): E. Roepke, Zeilweg 44, 60439 Frankfurt, Deutschland
Druck (Print): Books on Demand GmbH, In de Tarpen 42, 22848 Norderstedt, Deutschland

OFFIÇIAL CORRESPONDENCE

REGARDING THE EXISTENCE OF

COAL AND IRON

IN THE

PUNJAB.

PUBLIC WORKS DEPARTMENT PRESS.
O. T. CUTTER.
1859.

OFFICIAL CORRESPONDENCE

REGARDING THE EXISTENCE OF

COAL AND IRON

IN THE

PUNJAB.

From R. H. DAVIES, *Esquire, Secretary to the Government of Punjab, to Lieutenant Colonel* H. YULE, *Secretary to the Government of India, Public Works Department, Calcutta,—Nos.* 373—1819.

Lahore, 5th August 1859.

SIR,—I AM directed to enclose in original a letter and its enclosures this day addressed by order of the Hon'ble the Lieutenant Governor to Professor Oldham, of Calcutta, relative to certain researches for Coal and Iron in the Hills about Murree, which His Honour has recently caused to be instituted. The specimens have been forwarded this day to your address in two separate packets by banghy post.

2. I am to request that after the enclosures have been perused by His Excellency the Viceroy, they may be forwarded, with the specimens, to Professor Oldham for analysis.

3. It is of great importance to have a speedy reply from Professor Oldham, the Committee now being on the spot, and the Lieutenant Governor trusts there may be no delay in his reporting.

From R. H. DAVIES, *Esquire, Secretary to Government of Punjab, to Professor* OLDHAM, *Calcutta,—No.* 1818.

Lahore, 5th August 1859.

SIR,—THE Hon'ble the Lieutenant Governor has recently appointed a Committee for the purpose of examining and reporting on the existence of Coal and Iron in the Hills about Murree. The Committee have just furnished their first report, a copy of which I have the honour to annex. The specimens have been forwarded in two separate packets to the Secretary to the Government of India, Public Works Department, with a request that they may be forwarded to you with this letter.

2. His Honour will be much indebted to you if you will analyze these specimens and communicate the result at the earliest date possible. Should the specimens from the north-east face of Mount Nir prove to be Coal, as supposed by the Committee, it will be a great incentive to vigorous exertions. The Mountain is on the banks of the Jhelum River, and there is water carriage within a few hundred feet of the locality.

Proceedings of a Committee assembled by order of the Hon'ble Sir ROBERT MONTGOMERY, K. C. B., *Lieutenant Governor of the Punjab and its Dependencies, to examine and report upon certain deposits in ranges of Mountains around Murree, supposed to be Coal.*

PRESIDENT :

Major A. ROBERTSON, Offg. Supt., Lahore and Peshawur Road.

MEMBERS :

Captain H. C. JOHNSTONE, Surveyor, Derajhat.

     "   *H. P. BABBAGE, Assistant Commissioner, Murree.*

T. A. S. H. WILSON, Esquire, Assistant Engineer, Offg. Executive Engineer, Goojrat Division, Lahore and Peshawur Road.

THE Committee having assembled pursuant to order at the village of Bugla, about 12 miles from Murree, on Wednesday, the 20th day of July 1859, and having received the attached instructions from the Secretary to the Punjab Government, occupied from the 20th to the 29th July in visiting various localities where the deposits had been found, and report as follows :—

1st.—The deposits under the village of Bugla, two in number, and two others in the same ravine, but some miles further down, and all within a short distance of the bottom of the ravine, were found to be small isolated irregular masses of a substance which the Committee consider to be lignite ; all the specimens with one exception were completely dug out. The exception, a small irregular mass in the face of a cliff, was so similar to others dug out that the Committee did not deem it necessary to incur the expense of blasting it.

2nd.—A specimen, similar in all respects to those above referred to, was completely excavated from the side of the ravine between the villages of Bail and Chuckka.

3rd.—Under the villages of Bulannia and Bhun, in ravines, two other specimens were completely dug out; these the Committee also consider lignite.

4th.—A very thin vein, not exceeding one inch in thickness, and about 40 or 50 feet long, was examined about a mile to the north-east of the village of Kotlee. It is in the face of a sand-stone cliff, and was so insignificant that the Committee did not deem it necessary to incur expense in blasting it out.

5th.—On one of the spurs of Mount Nir, under the village of Thoon, a deposit was found in the face of an isolated rock ; it appeared so similar to others dug out, that nothing was done with it.   .   :

6th.—The examination of the specimens sent into Murree led the Committee to look with most confidence to the deposit on the south-east side of Mount Nir near the village of Kundole. Mount Nir seems to have been the centre of considerable disturbance. The main portion of the Mountain is formed of alternate layers of sand-stone and clay in nearly horizontal strata, having only a slight dip to W. S. W. A lower range, close to it on the south-east has the strata dipping to the north, almost at an angle of 45°. The ranges to the north parallel to Mount Nir, as far as and including the Murree range, have the strata dipping also to the north at from 30° to 35°, while the mountains to the east across the Jhelum River have the strata dipping only slightly to the east.

On the east face of Mount Nir,* about 800 or 1,000 feet above the

* About 20 miles south-east of Murree.

level of the River Jhelum, and at no great distance from the River, is situated the deposit above referred to. It is in an irregular vein at the foot of a sand-stone cliff, having a blue clay both above and below it. The main portion of the vein is about seven feet long, of an irregular form, 16 inches wide at the centre, and 8 inches at the ends, thus—

It shows again irregularly to the right and left, but much thinner, and altogether extends as far as can be seen about 30 feet in length. The deposit is mixed with slate, and appears to the Committee to be Coal of a fair quality.

No Member of the Committee possesses a sufficient knowledge of Geology to pronounce an opinion upon what may be expected from following up the vein, or whether it is most advisable to push the investigation by further search in the line of the vein above it or below it; Nor have they the means or manipulatory skill definitely to pronounce upon the real nature of the deposit. The test they have applied, and upon which their opinion as to its being Coal of fair quality is based is distillation, under which it yields gas which burns with a white clear flame, and Coal tar; but, as far as they could discover, no trace of acetic acid.

On the north-east spur of the Mountain, but a short distance from the site of the above deposit, but much higher up, a deposit is reported in the face of the sand-stone cliff. The specimen was brought in after the Committee had left. It has the appearance of Cannel Coal or Jet, being hard and polished, and not soiling the hand.

The Committee would recommend that the accompanying specimens of the deposits from Mount Nir, with the above description of the Mountain, be sent at once to Professor Oldham at Calcutta, and his opinion of the specimens and advice as to the best means of conducting the search be solicited. Meantime the Committee recommend that a boring be made from above, and about 60 feet back from the face of the cliff, at the foot of which the vein exists, to ascertain whether the vein extends back, and if so, if it increases in thickness. The Committee are also inclined to follow up the search by sinking shafts, as they look for thicker veins being found below, but they hope to be guided in this matter by Professor Oldham's opinion.

7th.—A large vein of black deposit is reported to exist in the bed of the Jhelum River, under the village of Kotlee, at present under water, but laid bare in the cold weather; this should be examined as soon as the river falls.

8th.—Wherever the deposit was found in rock the rock under was stained red by the wash from the vein. This the Committee believe shews the presence of some of the salts of Iron in all these deposits, probably the sulphuret.

· The Committee would also add that in the two latter specimens referred to in para. 1, what they consider iron pyrites was observed, and in the sand-stone close to the vein on the east face of Mount Nir traces of what they consider mica were discovered.

9th.—The Committee propose proceeding to visit other spots where deposits have been found, and will furnish reports in continuation.

From R. H. DAVIES, Esquire, Secretary to Government of Punjab and its Dependencies, to Professor OLDHAM, Calcutta,—No. 1963.

Lahore, 22nd August 1859.

SIR,—IN continuation of my letter No. 1818 of the 5th instant, I am directed to annex copies of two more reports of the Proceedings of the Committee appointed for ascertaining the existence of Coal and Iron in the hills about Murree. The specimens therein referred to have been forwarded for analysis by Bullock Train to the address of the Secretary to Government in the Public Works Department, through whom this letter will be forwarded to you.

2. The Hon'ble the Lieutenant Governor requests that you will be so good as to examine the specimens now sent, and give your opinion on them at as early a date as may be practicable.

Supplementary Proceedings (No. I.) of a Committee assembled by order of the Hon'ble Sir ROBERT MONTGOMERY, K. C. B., Lieutenant Governor of the Punjab and its Dependencies, for the purpose of ascertaining the existence of Coal and Iron Mines on the Murree Hills.

PRESIDENT :

Major A. ROBERTSON, Offg. Supt., Lahore and Peshawur Road.

MEMBERS :

Captain H. C. JOHNSTONE, Derajhat Survey.
   "   *H. P. BABBAGE, Assistant Commissioner, Murree.*

THE Committee having re-assembled at Derakote dutoon on Tuesday, the 9th day of August 1859, continued their examinations of various deposits supposed to be coal, until the 14th August, and report the result as follows :—

1st.—The Committee examined a deposit in the bottom of a ravine between Derakote and Chulavera. This was of small extent, and appeared of no value.

2nd.—In the great ravine under Chulavera, the Committee examined two specimens, one about 400 feet up the bank, and the other in the bottom of the ravine. Both specimens were in the face of sand-stone strata; these strata run nearly south-east and north-west, and dip to the south-west at about an angle of 75°, and the two specimens were in lines of sand-stone, only about 200 feet apart, and separated by layers of clay and indurated clay. The upper specimen was not in the form of a vein, but in an irregular hole in the rock, almost at right angles to the line of the strata; the deposit consisted of what appeared to the Committee a branch of a tree in a horizontal position, surrounded by a deposit resembling Coal. The branch was broken up in extracting it; but the pieces, together with a specimen of the rock and the surrounding deposit, are herewith sent.

The lower deposit was found in an irregular vein from 1 inch to 2 inches thick, running parallel to the strata but broken and very irregular; in some places, one vein only being visible, and in other parts two and three parallel ones; the whole extent exposed was about 30 feet in length. The deposit was in contact with clay, some of which appears to the Committee to contain iron; specimens of the deposit clay, contiguous rock, &c., &c., accompany.

3rd.—The next deposit was found close to the village of Bandie, a considerable distance up the hill, and was completely dug out; specimens are submitted.

4th.—The last specimen examined was under the village of Cheganah, in the bottom of the ravine, found in exactly the same description of rock as the second and third specimens, the direction of the strata being the same, but almost vertical instead of dipping to the south-west. The deposit was found in an almost square hole about 18 inches on the side, and in the line of the strata. Specimens of rock and deposit are submitted. The Committee would explain that all these specimens, as well as two referred to in last report, were found in one ravine or its branches, raising near the village of Kotlee and running in N. N. E. direction, until it joins the river Jhelum, under the village of Cheganah. The ravine is about eighteen or twenty miles long, and seven specimens have been found along it, all with one exception near the bottom.

The specimens examined by the Committee are all either isolated masses, or the veins so meagre, that, in their opinion, there is little inducement to incur expense in boring, or other examination, but they consider Professor Oldham should be consulted on the subject.

The Committee have now completed the examination of all specimens of supposed coal discovered and reported, and they purpose proceeding to-morrow to examine the Iron-mines at Bukkote, &c.

The Committee are of opinion that specimens (of Coal) should be found in the hills on the Kahoota Tuhseel, and would suggest the offering a reward in that Tuhseel, as also in Huzara.

Supplementary Proceedings (No. II.) of a Committee assembled by order of the Hon'ble Sir ROBERT MONTGOMERY, K. C. B., *Lieutenant Governor of the Punjab and its Dependencies, for the purpose of ascertaining the existence of Coal and Iron Mines on the Murree Hills.*

PRESIDENT :

Major A. ROBERTSON, *Offg. Supt., Lahore and Peshawur Road.*

MEMBERS :

Captain H. C. JOHNSTONE, *Derajhat Survey.*
 " H. P. BABBAGE, *Assistant Commissioner, Murree.*

THE Committee occupied from the 15th to the 17th in examining the Iron deposit at Bukkote. This Iron is found in the lime-stone formation ; is in the form of nodules embedded in clay; the clay appears an isolated deposit, not in the form of a vein; and the Committee do not feel themselves qualified to pronounce an opinion as to the supply, but no doubt Professor Oldham will be able to do so from an examination of the specimens accompanying, and the Committee are prepared to furnish any further information he may require.

The Committee obtained some information regarding Coal (near Bukkote) and two specimens herewith submitted, one of which much resembles plumbago, but the Committee did not follow up the search at the present time, as it appears no notice has been given to the people in Huzara, and they therefore thought it better to defer further researches until such time as the people have been told that rewards will be given. The Committee have taken upon themselves to offer a reward of five Rupees to any individual who points out a seam or vein, not less than twelve feet long and one and half inch thick. They also purpose, with His Honour's sanction, giving smaller rewards for any deposit pointed out.

The Committee will continue their researches as soon as they receive further information.

The Committee submit specimens of quartz found associated with the Iron deposit.

Note of Analysis of three specimens of Coal from " the Hills about Murree" received from the Under Secy. to Govt. of India, 30th August 1859.

No. 1 Coal.   36 per cent. of volatile matter.
              56 Carbon.
              8 Ash.

              —————
              100

No. 2 $30\frac{1}{2}$ per cent. of volatile matter.
              $45\frac{1}{2}$ of Carbon.
              24 Ash.

              —————
              100

No. 3   31 per cent. volatile.
              37 Carbon.
              32 Ash.

              —————
              100

The specimens are numbered 1, 2, and 3 respectively, for convenience, but the original labels were so much rubbed away, and injured by moisture during their transit, as to be almost entirely illegible. No. 3 is that specimen of which a very small quantity was sent in an envelope labelled " Cannel Coal Mount Nir."

2. With respect to Nos. 1 and 2 there ought to be no difficulty in recognizing the specimens to which the analyses refer, from the great

quantity of ash in No. 2, but the presence of this greater quantity of ash probably arises from the manner in which the specimens were selected. No. 2 being evidently chosen so as to include, along with what is really Coal, a thick layer of shale.

3. This shaly part was of course reduced to powder along with the rest, and an average of the whole taken for analysis; and thus an exaggerated and incorrect idea of the quantity of ash arrived at.

4. If the shaly portions of No. 2 be excluded, the composition of the remainder, or true Coal, resembles that of No. 1, as closely as if they had been broken from the same mass.

5. For all practical purposes the accompanying rough analyses will prove sufficient, but a more elaborate one could if necessary be made.

6. The volatile matter as above given is slightly excessive, for it includes the water, as also a small portion of the carbon, which latter element will of course appear proportionably less than it ought, the errors however due to these sources are very slight.

7. The nature of the volatile gases has not been investigated, nor have the several ingredients of the ash been estimated.

8. No trace of sulphur was detected, and the blocks of Coal have carried very well, crumbling very little, though from the torn condition of the wax cloth in which they were wrapt up, they had been evidently much shaken about.

J. G. MEDLICOTT,

Asst. in charge Geological Survey Office.

From Colonel R. BAIRD SMITH, *Offg. Secretary to the Govt. of India, P. W. Dept., to* R. H. DAVIES, *Esquire, Secretary to the Government of the Punjab,—No.* 6786.

Fort William, 27th September 1859.

SIR,—WITH reference to your letters Nos. 373—1819 and 404—1964, dated 5th and 22nd ultimo, I am directed to forward for the information of His Honour the Lieutenant Governor, a copy of the report received from the Geological Survey Office on the specimens of Coal forwarded with your letter of the 5th August.

2. The report is so encouraging and the discovery will be of such vast importance if the Coal is in workable quantity, that His Excellency the Governor General in Council has resolved on having the localities

examined by a competent and scientific Geologist, who will be able to furnish the Government with definite and reliable information, both on the scientific and economic conditions of the deposits. His Excellency has therefore selected for the duty Mr. H. Medlicott, the Professor of Geology in the Thomason College, a gentleman well qualified for the work, and in whose opinions on such a question His Lordship has every confidence.

3. Mr. Medlicott has been directed to proceed to Murree as early as practicable, and there to await the instructions of the Lieutenant Governor.

From THOMAS OLDHAM, *Esquire, Superintendent of Geological Survey of India, to Captain* A. FRASER, *Under Secretary to the Government of India, Public Works Department,—No. 297.*

The 3rd October 1859.

SIR,—ADVERTING to your letters No. 5995, dated 29th August 1859, and No. 6215, dated 5th September, together with the correspondence forwarded therewith, relating to the discovery of Coal in the vicinity of Murree, I have now the honour to report—

2. During my absence on duty in Madras, from whence I have only returned a few days, Mr. Medlicott, then in charge of this Office, took immediate steps to comply with the request of the Secretary to the Government of the Punjab, for an analysis of the specimens of Coal forwarded, and in his letter No. 294, dated the 21st ultimo, communicated to you the results adding a few remarks. From that communication, you will have perceived that so far as the *quality* of the minerals forwarded was concerned, they represented good useful fuel, on the whole better than the average quality of Indian Coal.

3. Mr. Medlicott did not enter on any discussion of the probable amount of supply, which would seem to be the most important question involved. On this point, I regret exceedingly, that, after a careful perusal of the Committee's reports, I cannot hold out any favourable hopes whatever. In their statement the Committee very plainly and succinctly give the fact, that in almost every instance where such Coal was observed they had *completely dug out the mass,* such as it was. In the only instances in which a vein or bed were seen, these were not more than a few inches in thickness, and very limited in length. From all·

the circumstances stated, it appears to me obvious that in all the places visited, the Committee have only met with repeated instances of what they themselves very justly suppose to have been the fact in one case, namely, of detached branches or stems of trees or small isolated accumulations of vegetable matter, imbedded in the sand-stones. In almost all such cases the bark of the tree is found converted into rich sparkling Coal, the stem or woody portion itself being often impregnated with coaly matter also. And I fancy that it is from such layers that the best specimens of Coal now forwarded have been obtained.

4. There is not, so far as I can see, anything in the reports of the Committee to warrant the supposition that true *beds* of Coal exist in that neighbourhood. There is, therefore, I conceive nothing at present known to justify the expenditure for shafts, &c., as suggested.

I may mention that precisely similar conditions occur in similar rocks, at the foot of the Sikkim Hills, on the Teesta and Sivok rivers (see my notes Journal Asiatic Society Bengal, Vol. XXIII (1854) p. 201). Large fragments of stems and branches of trees are there imbedded in the sand-stones, from which Coal of very promising quality was obtained, but which proved to be nothing more than isolated masses of no extent.

5. On the other hand, there is nothing in the geological facts of the case to render it impossible that widely extended beds of Coal should exist there, and it will be very desirable that the attention of the natives should be directed to the importance of the enquiry, and the communication of any knowledge on the subject of the occurrence of such Coal be stimulated by small rewards. I would beg that I may be kept acquainted with the results from time to time. And should there be anything to justify a well grounded hope of useful fuel being found, I shall be prepared, under the sanction of the Governor General in Council, to despatch one of my colleagues, or to proceed myself to examine the locality. I am confident that nothing yet reported on would justify the expenditure of time required for such an examination.

6. I would beg the favour of your forwarding this letter to the Secretary to Government of the Punjab, at your earliest convenience.

From T. OLDHAM, *Esquire, Superintendent of Geological Survey of India, to Captain* A. FRASER, *Under Secretary to Government of India, Public Works Department,—No.* 351.

The 19*th November* 1859.

SIR,—I HAVE the honour to acknowledge the receipt of the specimens from Murree of Coal &c., forwarded with your letter No. 7888, dated 15th November 1859.

These specimens have been examined, although I did not think that any of them demanded a chemical analysis ; they are in all respects similar to those formerly reported on.

The specimen labelled as " supposed by the Committee to be a portion of a tree" is so. It is a portion of a stem impregnated with silica, and so petrified, with minute strings of coaly matter attached.

———

From C. A. OLDHAM, *Esquire, in charge Geological Survey Office, to Captain* A. FRASER, *Under Secretary to Government of India, Public Works Department,—No.* 360.

The 7*th December* 1859.

SIR,—IN the absence from Calcutta of the Superintendent of the Geological Survey of India, I am instructed to forward to you the accompanying copy of the Report furnished to the Government of the Punjab by H. B. Medlicott, Esq., Geological Survey, on the reported Coal of Murree and of Kotlee.

———

From H. B. MEDLICOTT, *Esquire, Geological Survey of India, to* R. H. DAVIES, *Esquire, Secretary to Government of Punjab.*

Camp Murree, 7*th November* 1859.

SIR,—OWING, as I conjecture, to the great desire of Government, that Coal should be found within British Territory, what must be considered as the real business of my hurried deputation to the Punjab was not put into my hands for some time after my arrival at Murree. For the first twelve days I was engaged in visiting the localities examined by the Committee appointed by His Honour the Lieutenant Governor, as well as several other places reported by the natives since this Committee ceased to act. All these localities are in the hills of the Rawul Pindee District between the meridian of Murree and the river Jhelum. My researches here proving altogether unpromising, I asked to be shown the report by Mr. Calvert, an Assistant Engineer on the Punjab Railway, on a place in the Cashmere Territory not far from the Jhelum, in which report I was told Mr. Calvert asserted the existence of regular seams of good Coal. From this report and the file of papers connected with it, I perceived at once that the Coal in Jummoo, and the rocks with which it is associated, are entirely different in character, from what I had seen in the hills east of Murree. Had I seen this report in the first instance, I should have been satisfied by a much more cursory examination of the Murree rocks, but thinking the conditions of all were alike, I wished, in compliance with Mr. Oldham's instructions, to leave no place unseen. With the permission of Government I therefore proceeded at once to examine the Coal deposit near Kotlee in Jummoo. The discovery of Coal and the statements that have been published of its abundance in these hills, originated from Mr. Calvert's report. I may then preface my account by a concise relation of the circumstances connected with this discovery. Mr. Brunton, Chief Engineer of the Punjab Railway, accompanied by Major Medley and Mr. Calvert went to Jummoo in May or June 1859, for the purpose of enquiring into the possibility of procuring Coal in the Cashmere Territory. The Maha Rajah so far afforded them every encouragement; among a number of samples collected by his orders for their inspection, one was recognised as good Coal, the others were lignite. The examination of one locality of this lignite, at Aknore on the Chenab, was sufficient to satisfy Mr. Brunton of the uselessness of further enquiry respecting it : it occurs in very limited patches imbedded in massive sand-stone, and is, no doubt, similar to what I have seen in the Murree Hills. Mr. Calvert was deputed by Mr. Brunton to examine the locality from which the one good specimen was procured near Kotlee on the river Poonch, a tributary of the Jhelum. I need not repeat the details of Mr. Calvert's description ; it was such as to satisfy Mr. Brunton and Major Greathed of the quality and abundance of the Coal, so much so that the latter Officer recommended that no further survey or enquiry should be made regarding it until an exchange of Territory or some other arrangement for the extraction of the Coal could be agreed upon with the Maha Rajah, lest His Highness should become unreasonable in his demands.

Before discussing the Coal formation of Kotlee, I wish to explain the case of the Murree Hills, and in the hope of satisfying those who are not familiar with such subjects yet are unwilling to relinquish the hopes that have been raised, I would very briefly state the few simple facts upon which my opinion is founded. First, respecting the chemical or mineralogical question—the *quality*. The fossil substances used as fuel, and most of which are known by the generic name of "Coal," present every shade of composition, from that of wood to that of charcoal, which is approximately pure carbon : the process is one of carbonization, or more properly the escape and modification of the volatile elements of the vegetable substance ; the varieties thus presented are known as "peat," "lignite," "common bituminous coal" and "stone-coal" or "anthracite ;" it is more or less arbitrary, at what points of the scale these names are severally applicable ; for lignite and Coal proper, it is usual to draw the line between the Coals that do, and those that do not yield a hard cohesive coke and it has been found that this property of coking does not exist, or but very imperfectly exists when the volatile ingredients exceed about 25 per cent, or more generally the heating quality of Coal is in proportion to the degree of carbonization. As an attendant fact, in lignite the vegetable structure is still more or less visible. Lignites, however, form a valuable fuel, when better Coal cannot be procured. The geological facts affecting the *quantity* are equally simple. Vegetable substances become fossil (buried) in two ways, by accumulation in the place of their growth, and the covering over of such accumulations by sedimentary matter consequent upon the slow changes of level of the earth's surface ; or else, vegetable substances become shifted and deposited with other sedimentary matter. The most regular and continuous deposits of Coal are proved to have been formed in the former manner. The facts by which a Geologist is guided in a search for Coal are *directly* by the nature of the rocks, and the presence in them of vegetable impressions ; and *indirectly*, by noting a series of rocks in which Coal is known to occur in one locality, and by its position in that series he can infer the probable or possible presence of Coal in the same group of strata in other localities : moreover, he is enabled to follow out any particular bed by studying the amount and direction of the dislocations to which the series have been subject since its formation.

The Murree Coal is *lignite* ; a good specimen of it analyzed in the laboratory of the Geological Survey of India gave 36 per cent of volatile matter ; in all the specimens the woody fibre is recognizable. I have examined 18 localities, widely scattered through a considerable range of hills, and they all present the same features.

The Coal in each consists of the stems and roots of trees imbedded in the thick beds of soft sand-stone of the lower Siwalik formation, or the middle Tertiary period of Geologists. When the stem has been crushed, the whole 2 to 3 inches thick is lignite; in other cases, the core is mostly silicified (petrified) wood, the bark alone being pure lignite. I did not see any place where half a maund of this substance could be extracted.

It is certainly not *impossible* that at some place in the group, a sufficient accumulation of such materials may have been formed to make it worth working; but to *exhaust* this possibility would be the work of years; the specimens are not confined to any definite position in the formation, but scattered through a great thickness of strata, so that it would be almost a blind search through the whole. For such a search no method could be so good as that of offering a high reward among the inhabitants, whose daily occupations make them acquainted with every portion of the ground, for the discovery of a useful quantity of Coal. As for boring or trenching it would simply be incurring expense on the strength of the barest possibility. For this area alone we might I think rest upon the *probability* afforded by the uniformly unpromising character of so many widely distributed localities, but this judgment is much confirmed by the extensive experience of these same rocks throughout the length of British Himalayas, where attention has been turned to the point, and with the same result. I could show many places in the lower Siwalik rocks, between the Sutlej and Nepal, where precisely similar nests of lignite can be seen.

I now come to the Kotlee Coal. Captain Babbage and I had some trouble in finding the localities mentioned in Mr. Calvert's report, owing to an unaccountable mistake made by that gentleman in his sketch map, in which the ravine of the Hills with Dundela and Mohara is placed on the west instead of on the east of the Poonch, the main river flowing past Kotlee. Arrived at Dundela, however, we had no difficulty in recognizing the main features expressed in the drawings. In examining this case, I wish, as far as possible, to accept Mr. Calvert's data; there are some few spots marked on his plan as anthracite, and which I could not discover on the ground, but this hardly affects the general question.

The rocks in the immediate vicinity of Dundela are thin carbonaceous shales and grits, with earthy ferruginous lime-stones; among them is "the

bed or seam of Coal or anthracite, varying in thickness from one inch to nearly two feet, undulating in chambers or bunches, more than in a continuous
even seam." This is Mr. Calvert's description of the spot he selected, from
which to take his samples, and it may serve as a *favourable type* of all
that is actually visible. Now, as I remarked above, our *á priori* knowledge or direct observation (short of actually seeing good beds of Coal)
can be but very vague ; the rocks enumerated are no doubt such as are
frequently associated with Coal, but it were contrary to all experience to
establish a general rule to that effect. There is no kind of *necessary* con-
nection between the phenomena ; and numerous instances are recorded of
such rocks being extensively carbonaceous, as in this case, without proving of any value. Upon these facts alone, therefore, I am convincel that
no Geologist could confirm Mr. Calvert's conclusion " that a further exploration must result in the discovery of good beds of Coal." Among unknown
rocks these facts would certainly suggest a further exploration of the surface, but without such a search resulting in some thing more positive,
I should consider any mining operations as proposed by Mr. Calvert, to
be an unwarranted expenditure of money. But it may be that Mr.
Calvert bases his opinion upon the *indirect* evidence, which is, as I said,
of great importance. He speaks of the red rocks between Kotlee and
Dundela as "new red sand-stone," and of the rocks in which the Coal occurs,
" as carboniferous strata" and mountain lime-stone. If this be his reason-
ing, I can only say that his facts are incorrect, and his inference unsound.
The very strata he describes are thickly strewn with fossils *characteristic
of the nummulitic formation,* which is of the lower Tertiary period,
and do not belong to a Palœozoic or Mesozoic group, as he assumes ; but
even if these rocks were of the carboniferous period, it were very rash,
at such a distance from any known Coal measures of that age, to specu-
late upon their yielding Coal. In point of fact indirect evidence is
entirely on the other side. From a close comparison of these rocks, with
the descriptions given in Dr. Flemming's report on the salt range (published in vol. 22 for 1853 of the Journal A. S. Bengal) I have no doubt
that these Coal measures are the same as what is there (p. 340) described as " lignite or salt range Coal." I saw no indications to make me
think the measure had been more favourably developed here than there ;
the resemblance is borne out even in some minute particulars. Dr.
Flemming's account is very circumstantial ; sufficiently so I should think to
settle the general question of value. Throughout a length of 130 miles

the conditions are uniform, one or two irregular discontinuous seams of Coal in carbonaceous alum-shales. He gives some instances of attempts to work it, and his report would be a most useful aid to any one undertaking further experiments. What was at first but a want of positive evidence in favour of useful beds of Coal at Dundela, thus becomes a case of decided probability against it. On every point the comparison is equally against any experiment at Dundela. Even if salt range Coal were of established value, the Geological conditions at Dundela are such as would make the extraction of it very uncertain ; these rocks are only brought to the surface there along a very narrow line of elevation ; the softer strata are so crushed up that the run of any individual bed could not be depended on for ten yards at a time. Geographically, Dundela is more inaccessible than any part of the salt range, and it is, moreover, in independent Territory.

In respect of composition, it is not improbable that in this place, it may have attained a higher degree of carbonization than in the salt range, but mechanically it seems to have suffered proportionably ; it is in a very fragmentary state. I have not delayed my report until I could, on my return to Roorkee, make a proper analysis of the Coal, but I have forwarded two specimens to Calcutta for this purpose.

In fine, it is my unhesitating opinion, *that the rocks at Dundela give no prospect of a useful supply of Coal.*

As regards Iron, I did not see anything at Dundela that deserves to be called an ore : that which the natives work very near at Moharee is very poor compared to most Indian ores.

It is a concretionary hæmatite (red oxide) but very imperfectly separated from the clays, both locally and in the mass, which is irregular in size and direction ; being apparently consequent upon the contortion and modification of the carbonaceous and ferruginous shales ; its occurrence is very uncertain, much of what the natives work being found in isolated patches in the hard lime-stone.

It is much to be regretted that the expectations of Government and of the Public should have been so needlessly excited : and it is equally to be wondered at that this could have been effected by such a document as Mr. Calvert's report, a single perusal of which could not fail to suggest grave doubts to any one who was competent to give an opinion in the matter.

I think it probable that localities similar to Dundela may be found in our own Territory, as I have noticed that the nummulitic rocks come to the surface again along a line west of Murree.

I will investigate this further before I leave the Hills.

Additional Report by H. B. MEDLICOTT, Esquire.

AFTER my return to Murree from the Jummoo Territory, there were still two places, Bukkote and Shah Durrah, reported by the natives as "Coal localities," and that I had not seen. From their position I thought that both might be representatives of what I had seen at Dundela; a sample from Shah Durrah confirmed this opinion; the Bukkote locality did not prove as I expected; it is, like all the previous cases in the Murree District, a broken thread of lignite in massive soft sand-stone.

At Shah Durrah, the section is very like that at Dundela. Soft carbonaceous shales cropping out along the base of a lime-stone ridge, and between this and a band of red sand-stones and clays. I did not succeed in getting a sound specimen of the Coal, even by digging into the bank; the man who had procured the sample said that the place had since then been set on fire, and, indeed, it had all the appearance of having undergone slow combustion; there was much sulphureous efflorescence about the surface. The villagers stated that small quantities of sulphur had formerly been extracted at this spot. This fact is a further point of identification with the beds already described in the salt range; in parts of the salt range, sulphur is obtained from the same set of beds as the lignite. Although the actual show of Coal at the surface is not so great at Shah Durrah as at Dundela, I would have just as little confidence of obtaining a supply from one place as from the other. The question is then brought back to the salt range, where it has already been so often discussed.

In compliance with instructions from Lahore, I accompanied Mr. Brunton to see the old Coal diggings at the base of the hills near the village of Seilah; as no satisfactory opinion could be formed from the inspection of a single locality, I spent some days, after Mr. Brunton's return to Lahore, in examining the rocks at other places. I trust that the following conclusions may be depended on, as far as facts are required. I need not add to those published in Dr. Flemming's report; it would be easy of course to lengthen the list of places where the Coal shales come to the surface, but this would be nothing to the purpose. Dr. Flemming has, if any thing, given too favourable an opinion.

The first question commonly suggested is, may we not expect more by boring or shaft sinking ? In respect of the *quantity* to be found, I think this admits of a most unequivocal negative answer, as is very easily understood by the following considerations : The complicated disturbance and subsequent excavation to which these rocks have been subjected, were such as to expose, repeatedly, and in every direction, the entire series of strata ; now, let it be recollected that Coal occurs in beds, not in lodes or veins, and that therefore, every part of these now exposed surfaces, the Coal bed among the rest, was once as deeply buried as is at present its continuation into the heart of the range ; thus, by boring we should only take one additional section of the series of which we have already such a great number, naturally exposed to day-light. Without a single exception, these natural sections are unpromising ; they show that the Coal, though. occurring with but little interruption, over a very large area, is no where of sufficient thickness, or sufficiently constant at a moderate thickness, to give a certainty of an abundant supply.

With the intention of testing its *quality*, I should be equally against going to any direct expense. I believe that the depth of 20 or 30 feet from the outcrop would give a fair sample of what might be expected all through ; and the native mine we visited extended to a much greater depth from the surface.

There still remains the question as to whether this Coal, such as it is, had not better be worked methodically, than left to the crooked devices of the natives. The answer to this had better be postponed. The economy of systematic works would not be felt for a long time after commencing operations. Such a poor seam as this might never repay much outlay in working it ; besides, it still remains to be seen if the stuff is workable at any price. I have no doubt that the natives, if left to themselves, would turn out a large quantity of Coal at a cheaper rate than under European Superintendence, and it is in this way that I would suggest the experiment to be made ; indeed, this is what Mr. Brunton at once determined upon doing when he had seen the mine near Seilah. With proper precautions, I think this course will give the means of deciding whether any thing more can be done or is worth doing. Mr. Brunton told me that a native had offered to deliver the Coal at Mooltan for eight annas a maund ; looking at it first as an experiment, I would not be inclined to drive a bargain ; a good price would be a principal means of procuring the best that is to be had ; the chief difficulty will be to free the Coal from the shale with which it is associated, and into which it graduates ; if the price is low, no trouble will be taken to effect this, and the first object of the trial might thus be frustrated.

Before any experiment at regular mining is undertaken, should such hereafter prove advisable, it were most desirable in the first instance to have a detailed Geological examination and map made of the entire area. This would require some considerable time ; and I do not think that the Geological Survey of India is prepared to undertake it during this season. But I beg respectfully to warn the Government of entrusting such an experiment to a man whose only qualification may be a familiarity with the use of the pick, or experience in the trade of shaft sinking. I have so often in India seen mistakes of this kind made, that I think it my duty, as a servant of Government, to give a caution when I have an opportunity.

In the foregoing report, I have throughout endeavoured to make my facts and reasons intelligible to those not familiar with such subjects, believing that this was expected from me ; it would have been easy to express my opinion in as many lines as I have taken pages.

Having now, in a manner, completed the several direct commissions on which I was deputed to the Punjab, I return to the work I was previously engaged in.

From C. A. OLDHAM, *Esquire, Assistant in charge Geological Survey Office, to Captain* A. FRASER, *Under Secretary to Government of India, Public Works Department,—No. 362.*

The 19*th December* 1859.

SIR,—IN the absence from Calcutta of the Superintendent of the Geological Survey, I am instructed to forward to you the annexed memorandum of the analysis of two additional specimens of Coal, received from H. B. Medlicott, Esq. The general character of the Coal is that of a hard anthracite.

Analysis of 2 *specimens of Coal from Kotlee, Punjab.*

No. 1.			No. 2.		
Carbon	90 5	per cent.	Carbon	90	per cent.
Volatile matter...	4 0	"	Volatile	6	"
Ash...	5 5	"	Ash	4	"